Journey Through the Fairy Door

By Mitchel Maree
Illustrations by Ola Snimshchikova

Other books in the
Magic Cube Series:

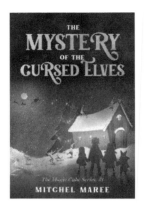

The Mystery of the Cursed Elves
Book #1

For Joe

Leader, mentor, friend. Forever in our hearts.

Text Copyright © 2021 Mitchel Maree
Illustration Copyright © 2021 Ola Snimshchikova

First paperback edition July 2021
ISBN **978-1-7360656-1-7** (paperback)

Contents

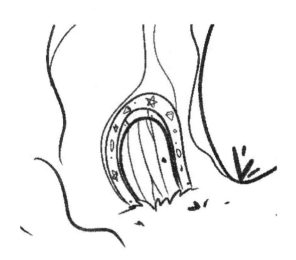

Chapter One

Discovery in the Woods

"I'm so bored," ten-year-old Sophie Watson whined. "Can we please go to the park?"

Dad turned from his computer to look out the window. "I suppose we could all use some fresh air," he said, stretching. "Round everyone up."

Sophie let out a whoop of joy before running around the house, yelling, "We're going to the park!"

Max, the eldest, switched off the computer game he was playing and searched out his shoes. Max loved outdoor adventures even more than video games.

"Everyone, get ready for the park!" Sophie continued shouting.

"Okay, okay! You don't have to yell." Violet emerged from the playroom with her hands covering her ears. Violet, the middle child, was much quieter than her older sister. Sophie's take-charge personality sometimes came off as loud and bossy. Still, she had a tender heart and always looked after her siblings.

Parker, the youngest, came bolting down the stairs at full speed. "The park! The park!" she yelled. She burst through the kitchen and into the mudroom to get her shoes.

Parker was fearless. Although her adventurous free spirit often clashed with Sophie's protective nature, Parker loved her sister dearly.

As soon as they were ready, the children burst through the door heading down the street toward the park. Their parents trailed farther and farther behind as the children raced ahead through the neighborhood.

"I'm going to the zipline," Max called out as soon as the playground came into view.

"I'm doing the monkey bars," Sophie said.

"Race you to the slide!" Parker challenged Violet, and off they all went.

Mom and Dad found an empty park bench to sit and watch their children scramble around the playground, laughing and teasing one another.

After several minutes, Max felt restless

with the zipline. "Who wants to climb some trees?" he suggested.

"I do!" Sophie answered. The other two quickly nodded in agreement.

They raced across the playground toward a patch of trees. Max climbed halfway up his favorite tree before the girls arrived below him, panting for breath. Sophie and Parker recovered quickly, instantly grabbing branches and hauling themselves up after Max.

Violet was much more interested in the budding flowers; she had no desire to compete with her siblings.

Crouching low, Violet investigated the flowers surrounding the trees. Red, orange, and yellow blossoms struggled to break through buds just beginning to open. Out of the corner of her eye, she caught a faint twinkling. Crawling through the grass, she searched for the source of the twinkle. A small fairy door hung loosely on the trunk of a large oak tree. The pink door was decorated in gems of various shapes and sizes— flowers, hearts, circles, diamonds, and squares. The jewels sparkled as the sunlight danced across them.

"I found a fairy door!" Violet squealed.

"I want to see." Sophie jumped down from the branches.

"Me too! Me too!" Parker practically slid down the tree trunk behind her sister.

Finding fairy doors dotted through the neighborhood was a favorite pastime of the Watson family. These small doors often came with several accessories helping to create a magical feeling for passersby. Tiny tables,

wishing wells, glittery mushrooms, and even tiny toy bicycles helped bring the imagination to life. This door was no exception.

"Look at how it sparkles," Sophie commented, leaning in to take a closer look.

As they stood studying the door, Max caught movement out of the corner of his eye.

"What is that?" he yelled as the object flew directly over their heads. Max instantly reacted by whacking violently into the air. "That bug is huge."

"Wait!" Violet grabbed at his arm. "It looks like a baby bird; maybe it fell out of its nest."

The creature circled back toward the children. Instinctively, they ducked, covering their heads. With his head down,

Max continued blindly whacking at the air above him.

"I think I got it," Max yelled. "Something hit my hand, and it bounced over that way."

"Oh, no!" Violet hurried in the direction Max pointed. "I hope you didn't kill it."

"There! I see something." Parker knelt in the grass, leaning in. "It's colorful. It could be a giant butterfly."

"It looks too big to be a butterfly," Violet told her. "With its wing covering the body, I can't make out what it is."

Parker and Violet leaned further forward, quickly jerking back as the creature flew up towards them.

"A fairy!" Violet gasped. The creature now hovered in front of the younger girls.

Violet had been right; the fairy was no bigger than a small bird. Bright shades of pink and purple swirled around both wings. The fairy lifted an arm, motioning for the girls to follow her as she flew toward the fairy door. As they watched in fascination, the fairy placed a tiny key into the small, pink door. The door sprung open, and the fairy disappeared inside.

"Should we follow her?" Violet asked with a shrug.

"How are we going to fit through there?" Sophie gave her a look of annoyance, gesturing toward the tiny opening in the tree trunk.

Parker ignored them and crawled toward the door. Reaching her hand inside, she felt around until her fingers touched the surface of something hard. She pulled the object out.

"The magic cube!" Max shouted excitedly, taking it from his sister's hand.

The cube had a large lever on top, buttons on one side, and switches on another. The last time they'd found the magic cube, it had transported them to the North Pole.

"Wait, shouldn't we think about this first?" Sophie asked, reaching to grab the cube from Max. "You know what happened last time."

"Of course, I remember." Max moved the cube out of Sophie's reach. "We had an awesome adventure."

Before she could stop him, Max pressed buttons, flipped switches, and pulled the lever up and down. There was a sudden burst of light, followed by complete darkness as if a cloud had moved across the sun. Seconds later, the sun was shining again as if nothing had happened.

Parker looked back through the fairy door,

surprised to see swirls of colorful light where there had been only darkness seconds earlier. The lights reminded her of stars dancing through the galaxy. Curious, she reached her hand inside once more. Instantly, the entrance stretched up and over, creating a doorway they could all easily fit through. Without a second thought, Parker scrambled up and ran through the opening.

"Too late now." Max gave a sly smile as he followed his youngest sister through the door.

"Come on." Violet tugged Sophie's arm. "What's the worst that can happen?"

"I guess we're about to find out," Sophie mumbled.

Chapter Two

Through the Fairy Door

They emerged from the door and found themselves in a field of thick, waist-high grass. The trees towered overhead, bending and curving to create a long tunnel in front of them.

"Parkour!" Max shouted, scrambling to climb one of the large set of boulders scattered along the side of the tunnel. After

scaling one large rock, he jumped across to the next boulder and then another. Taking a break, he scanned the trees surrounding them. Some branches hung low near the ground, circling around the trees like a ladder, climbing toward the sky. "I dare you to climb one of those trees, Parker."

"I dare you," Parker shot back, struggling to climb onto one of the boulders.

"You be careful, Parker," Sophie warned, wincing when Parker's foot slipped from the rock.

Parker slid the short distance back to the ground before moving to try her luck at a different rock.

Out of nowhere, Sophie began wiggling and squirming. "My back itches."

"Mine too," Parker said, giving up on climbing the rocks. Instead, she leaned her back against the boulder, moving up and down as if it were a scratching post.

"It's so itchy." Sophie wiggled around, stretching one arm behind her but unable to reach the itch. "Scratch it! Scratch it!" She turned her back towards Violet, begging for help.

"It's tickling me," Parker laughed as she squirmed about. "Is there something crawling on me?"

Violet reached out to scratch at Sophie's back but stopped short when they heard a tearing sound.

"Did my shirt just rip?" Sophie strained her neck, trying to see.

"Ahhh!" Violet yelled, jumping back, and pointing. "What is that?"

"What? Is it a bug?" Sophie screeched, shaking herself while jumping up and down.

"Get it off! Get it off!"

Max jumped down from the rocks and rushed over to Sophie, curious to learn what the yelling was about. Sure enough, Sophie's shirt had two rips over both shoulder blades. Two blue specks poked out of the newly made holes. As if attached to a spring, two bright blue wings popped out of Sophie's back. Max managed to jump back in time to avoid being smacked in the face.

At that exact moment, Parker heard her shirt rip. "What the heck? This shirt is brand new. Mom is going to freak."

Parker's concern was quickly forgotten when two purple wings sprang out through each tear. She whipped her head from side to side, examining the wings. "Whoa! Cool!"

"Wings!" Violet yelled, looking from one set of wings to the other. "You both have wings!"

No sooner had the words been spoken when more ripping sounds were heard. Violet and Max looked at each other, excitement dancing in their eyes. Within seconds, wings sprung out from behind them both. Violet's a brilliant pink, while Max's were a swirling orange and black.

"This is so cool!" Parker exclaimed. "Can we fly? Oh, I bet we can fly!"

"We just need to figure out how these work." Max shrugged his shoulders, attempting to move the wings up and down.

"We probably need fairy dust." Violet's brows furrowed in thought. "That's how they do it in books."

"Maybe if we think happy thoughts," Sophie suggested.

"Imagine you're flying, and you will," a

soft voice said from behind them.

The kids turned around and came face to face with the fairy they had seen earlier.

"Hi," she said with a wave. "I'm Pixie."

"You grew," Violet commented, noticing they were now the same size as the fairy.

"Actually, you shrank." Pixie smiled.

"That's why everything looks gigantic," Parker smacked her forehead with the palm of her hand.

"Ummm, sorry about whacking you earlier," Max mumbled, staring at the ground.

"Don't worry about it." Pixie waved him off. "So, are you ready to fly?"

Max and Sophie looked at one another, their eyes widening.

"I'm ready! I'm ready!" Parker said, jumping up and down. "How do we do it?"

"Its' simple, really. Picture yourself flying, and you will," Pixie explained. "Don't think about anything else, except flying right here next to me."

She flew up into the air and hovered there with hands stretched out, inviting them into the empty spaces next to her.

Max looked up at Pixie and tried to picture himself next to her, but nothing happened. He jumped a few times, then concentrated on flapping his wings, but still, he did not fly.

Violet had the most vivid imagination. For her, it was simple; she took one look at Pixie and, in an instant, fluttered up, squealing with delight.

Never one to be outshined, Parker imagined herself flying even higher than Violet. Much to her surprise and delight, Parker rose into the air.

20

"I'm flying! I'm flying!" she yelled, floating higher and higher. Parker shot across the sky, dipping down, soaring back up, turning circles in the air, and laughing. "It's so easy!"

"Be careful," Sophie warned, feeling dread in her stomach. She would never hear the end of it if something happened to Parker. "You need to slow down."

"You're flying." Parker raised her eyebrows and pointed down.

Sophie gasped; how had she gotten up here? Fearing she might fall, she forced herself to concentrate on Parker swishing back and forth next to her. Instead of helping her relax, she felt a little sick. Violet reached out and took Sophie's hand, helping ease her panic.

Still stuck on the ground, Max felt frustrated; it wasn't fair how easy it looked for his sisters to fly. He furrowed his brows and clenched his fists while jumping up. Nothing happened.

"You're trying too hard," Pixie said gently, landing next to him. "You're overthinking it. There isn't any logic to it. Simply picture yourself flying, and let your body lift you up."

"Like walking," Sophie said, floating a few feet above him. "You don't think about how to move your legs. You just know where you want to go, and your brain does the rest for you."

Max took a deep breath and concentrated on a spot next to Sophie, telling himself that's where he wanted to be. Finally, he felt himself lift off the ground.

"I did it," he said, his face lighting up. "I guess I was overthinking it."

"Now that you can get up, let's learn how to land," Pixie said. "It's the same concept. Picture where you want to be, hover over your landing spot, point your toes, and let your foot touch the ground. The rest of your body will follow."

The children followed Pixie down to the ground and copied her movements until they stood next to her.

"Now practice taking off and landing a few times," Pixie said.

After practicing for a few minutes, the children could take off, fly, and land with no problems.

"It's easy once you get the hang of it," Max commented. "And don't overthink it."

"You've got it," Pixie said. "Now, follow

me. We're off to Emerald Valley."

"What's Emerald Valley?" Sophie asked.

Pixie laughed. "The home of the fairies, of course."

Chapter Three

Emerald Valley

They flew single file down the avenue of trees until it opened into a large forest. They fanned out, weaving in and out of trees, dipping low, and flying back up.

"This is the best day ever!" Parker shouted.

When they flew out of the trees, the ground seemed to disappear from beneath them. Max glanced behind him to see they had flown off a cliff. A large mountain loomed in front of them. Below lay a deep ravine. Pixie made a downward motion with her arm and led the descent toward the valley below.

Near the bottom of the canyon, a small forest ran along the right side of the bank. Pixie led them through a large cluster of green trees, which opened into a massive clearing. The children gasped as they moved from vibrant living trees to what looked like a desert.

They came in for a landing on a pile of brown, crunchy leaves. Everything was brown, dried up, and looked dead. Clusters of small trees and bushes stood bare, the last of their brown leaves clinging to hold on. A dried riverbed ran the length of the valley, ending in a pool of gooey mud. Exposed tree roots were covered in shriveled brown moss.

The ground looked cracked as if it would break open at any moment. Near the far side of the clearing, a group of blackened trees stood surrounded by ash, the faint smell of smoke still lingering in the air.

"This is it?" Sophie asked, wrinkling her nose.

"Doesn't shout emerald to me," Parker announced bluntly.

Pixie looked over her shoulder, glaring at Parker.

"What? It's true." Parker shrugged and held up her hands.

"Something bad must have happened here," Violet said, tapping her chin and walking around like a detective from one of her storybooks. "Emerald Valley doesn't usually look like this, does it?"

"No." Pixie shook her head slowly.

"Emerald Valley is dying."

"I think that ship has sailed," Parker said flatly. "This place is dead."

"Parker," Sophie hissed.

"She's right," Pixie said, dropping her eyes and lightly kicking at the ground. "Without the fairy queen's magic, our home is fading away."

"Fairy queen?" Violet's ears perked up.

"Her magic is what keeps this place alive," Pixie told them. "Now, she's missing."

"What happened?" Sophie asked, concern filling her eyes.

"Every morning, the fairies gather for a breakfast meeting," Pixie began. "We discuss chores and plans for the day. One morning about two weeks ago, Queen Buttercup didn't show up for breakfast. She always shows up; she leads the meetings. We didn't know what to do or where to look. It was as if she'd vanished into thin air. Without the queen, the river stopped flowing, and things began to wilt and die. Then the giants and dragons came."

Max stopped in his tracks. "The what and the who, now?"

"Giants and dragons." Parker threw her hands up. "Pay attention."

Max rolled his eyes.

"The dragons came and burned half our village down," Pixie continued, pointing to the row of scorched trees. "The giants came next, snatching fairies. Everyone panicked. It took all the water left in the lake to put the fires out."

"Where did they take the fairies?" Sophie asked. "And why?"

"We don't know," Pixie said. "The

dragons have come back twice now. Luckily, they didn't burn anything, but they keep taking fairies. All the remaining fairies have gone into hiding, deep underground. They're too afraid to come outside. Things are getting bad here, so I went to find help. I found you four."

"So, you want us to fight giants and dragons?" Max was skeptical. "That might be too much for us to handle. We don't have any weapons, and we're just kids."

"Hopefully, we don't need weapons." Pixie flinched at the thought. "I need help finding Queen Buttercup. It's the only way we can save Emerald Valley."

"What about the giants and the dragons?" Max couldn't stop thinking about them.

Before anyone could answer, the sky turned dark as a large shadow passed over them. Pixie froze in place, straining her ears. The children looked up, scanning the sky.

"Shh." Pixie placed a finger to her lips.

A loud crack echoed through the valley, the sound of branches breaking in half. Another sound, like the whistling of a windstorm, filled the air. More branches snapped, followed by a piercing screech. The ground trembled and shook beneath them.

"What's happening?" Sophie's voice trembling in fear.

A sudden wind whipped around them, blowing dirt and dead leaves up from the ground. The wind grew in intensity, slamming into the children and knocking them to the ground. They imagined this is what a hurricane must feel like.

"Dragons!" Pixie screamed.

"We have to run!" Max scrambled along

the ground, struggling to stand up.

"I can't move!" Parker yelled. Desperately she tried to get up on her hands and knees, but the wind held her down.

Sophie screamed as a large dragon broke through the trees. Its powerful flapping wings bringing more of the wind and keeping them pinned to the ground. Two more dragons dropped from the sky and headed straight for the children.

While one dragon continued flapping its wings, a second dragon stretched out its sharp claws and wrapped them around Sophie, lifting her kicking and screaming into the air.

"Help!" tears stung Sophie's eyes as fear knotted in her stomach.

"Sophie!" Max struggled to reach up and

grab his sister.

The third dragon screeched loudly as it swooped down to capture Max. Reaching out its other scaly arm, it grabbed Violet and soared back up into the sky. The remaining dragon caught Pixie and Parker and joined the other two in the air.

"Don't look down," Max warned a trembling Violet.

They soared out of the trees and along the ravine before quickly heading up and away from Emerald Valley.

Parker held a hand over her face but couldn't help peeking through her fingers at the dragon.

As always, curiosity got the best of her. She reached out to touch the creature's scaly skin and shivered at the feel of it. It was rough and bumpy and thick.

At first glance, the dragons had looked black, but with the sunlight bouncing off the scales, their color changed to a dramatic midnight blue.

Parker glanced ahead, surprised by how quickly they were approaching a mountain. She could just make out the tiny entryway they were speeding directly toward.

"We aren't going to make that!" Parker yelled into the wind.

It was too late. The dragons were coming in too fast to stop now. Parker squeezed her eyes shut and braced for a crash landing.

Chapter Four

Caged

Seconds before the dragons crashed into the side of the mountain, their bodies turned sideways to glide perfectly through the archway and into a vast cave.

Parker squealed as the dragons straightened out only to turn, speeding up one tunnel, through another, before making a sharp right turn into yet another tunnel. Her tummy dropped like it did on carnival rides. Parker let out a tiny giggle.

Finally, the dragons coasted over a clear pool of water before coming to a stop inside a dimly lit cavern. Each dragon floated down slowly to land, careful not to harm their prey. Once landed, their claws opened, and the prisoners were freed.

"What is this place?" Max questioned in awe, daring to stand up.

"Blazing Peak," Pixie whispered in reply. "Somewhere in here is the portal to the Vatrena Dolena, the valley of fire."

"Valley of fire?" Parker squealed with delight, immediately slapping a hand over her mouth.

"The land of dragons." Pixie nodded toward their kidnappers.

"Is that where they're taking us?" Violet asked, still trembling as a shiver ran down her spine.

The dragons sat calmly, pecking at each other playfully and biting at their own tails. They seemed to have little interest in their captives.

"Perfect," a gruff voice came from the shadows in front of them.

"It's a giant," Sophie squeaked as the figure stepped into view.

The dragons flapped their massive wings. Max winced, nervous the dragons would grab them again. But, instead, the dragons flew up toward the top of the cave. Max could just make out a ledge where the dragons landed. He noticed several shadows moving along the ridges and wondered how many dragons were up there.

"So good of you to join us," the giant's voice echoed through the cave as he took heavy steps toward them.

41

The giant walked with a slight limp. A black cape hung around his shoulders. He grabbed the sides of the hood and pulled it down to reveal his face. The children looked at one another in surprise. Although he towered over Max, the giant didn't look much older than their brother.

In his hands, he carried a large birdcage. In one quick movement, he set the cage on the ground and scooped the prisoners inside it. Once the door was securely closed, the giant carried them further into the cave. The cage swung back and forth as the giant limped along; the passengers inside slid from one side to the other.

"I think I'm going to be sick." Sophie covered her mouth with one hand while grabbing her stomach with the other.

Finally, the jostling stopped. The giant

hung the cage on a large hook jutting out of the wall.

"Welcome to your new home," he chuckled, pressing his face against the bars to peer in at them. "The lady will be along soon, so rest up. She'll be wanting your magic."

"Is everyone okay?" Pixie whispered once the giant was out of view.

"Did we just get kidnapped by dragons?" Sophie asked.

"Pretty much," Parker said, pushing herself off the cage floor and running her fingers along the cold, metal bars.

Parker stopped at the door studying it. Grabbing the metal poles with both hands, she shook violently. When that did nothing, she reached her hand through, searching for a latch.

"There has to be a way out of here," she

muttered, sliding her leg between the poles.

"I wouldn't do that," Max warned. "Remember when you got your head stuck in the banister?"

Parker shot him a dirty look but stopped trying to squeeze her way through the bars. As her eyes slowly adjusted to the darkness, Parker noticed they weren't alone.

"Hey, guys." she motioned them over. "Look out there."

Max, Sophie, Violet, and Pixie hurried over to Parker, looking out where she pointed. Cages, identical to theirs, hung all around the room.

"Hello?" Pixie yelled. "Hello? It's Pixie. Is anyone out there?"

"Pixie! Pixie!" several voices called out from different cages.

"It's them," Pixie turned toward the

children in excitement. "It's the other fairies! Is everyone all right?" she turned back toward the cages.

"We're not hurt," a voice nearby answered.

"Axel? Is that you?" Pixie asked.

"Yeah, hi," Axel said, peering out the side of the cage next to them.

"Oh, Axel! It's so good to see you," Pixie said. She turned to quickly explain, "Axel lives next door to me. He's been missing for a week now."

The children nodded as more fairies came to the front of their cages and stared at the newcomers.

"Is everyone here?" Pixie asked. "Where is Queen Buttercup? Is she here?"

"She's up there." Axel pointed toward the ceiling.

Pixie and the children leaned against the bars of their cage and looked up. Above them, a single cage hung high in the center of the room. It was impossible to see inside.

"She's in pretty bad shape," Axel said with a frown. "The giants have taken most of her magic. Now they want to steal ours."

"That explains why Emerald Valley is dying," Pixie said. "The queen's magic keeps the valley alive. Without her, we don't stand a chance of saving our home."

"We'll save her," Violet promised, placing a hand on Pixie's shoulder. "We'll save everyone."

"There's no way out of here," Parker told her sister. "Look at the other cages; they all have locks. We need a key to unlock the doors."

"The giants have the key," Axel told them.

"Are there only two of them?" Max questioned. "Giants, I mean."

"Yes, the boy and a woman," Axel confirmed. "The woman is in charge; she's the one who steals the magic. The boy does whatever she tells him to do. He keeps the key in his pocket."

Max looked up at the ceiling and watched the shadows moving along the wall, "Do those dragons ever leave?"

"Nope. They're like watchdogs," Axel replied. "I think the giants use magic to control the dragons."

"Even more reason to save the queen," Violet said. "We need to rescue the fairies and free the dragons!"

Chapter Five

Giants and Dragons

"Giants, dragons, and fairies? What's next? Unicorns?" Sophie grabbed her head with her hands dramatically.

"I want to meet the unicorns!" Violet said, clapping her hands together quickly.

The sound of approaching footsteps and light murmurs interrupted the conversation. Two giants emerged from the darkness into the dimly lit cave. The boy carried a wide tray loaded with food: a loaf of bread, a pile of spaghetti, huge meatballs, and a pitcher.

"I'm starving." Parker licked her lips and rubbed her tummy. Her stomach gave a loud growl at the sight of food.

"How can you even think of eating right now?" Sophie asked in disgust. "My stomach is so full of knots I couldn't eat if I tried. Not to mention, that bread is bigger than your head."

"I want to climb on top of that loaf of bread and start gnawing at it," Parker said through gritted teeth. "You know how I feel about food. If I sees it, I eats it."

Sophie rolled her eyes.

The boy set his tray down on a table, standing in the middle of the room.

"Caught a few more, we did," he said proudly while ripping the bread into small pieces.

"Good. I need as many as we can capture," the woman replied, reaching up to unhook the cage holding Queen Buttercup. "This one is running out of magic."

She set the cage down on the table next to the food and peered in at the fairy queen.

Turning to the boy, she grunted, "Give me some water."

The boy quickly poured water from the pitcher into a thimble and handed it to the woman.

"Drink up, Your Majesty." The woman opened the cage and thrust the cup toward the fairy.

"She doesn't look so good," the boy muttered, taking a knife to cut the pasta.

"She'll be fine," snapped the woman. "We just need to force some water and food down her throat. I need *her* to get the magic out of the rest of these fairies."

The woman stared into the cage for several seconds. Queen Buttercup didn't move from where she lay. The woman slammed the door in frustration.

"She won't drink," she spat out.

"Food is ready to be served." The boy held up the tray proudly, ignoring her comment.

With a grunt, the woman returned Queen Buttercup's cage to its hanger in the middle of the room. Taking the key the boy held out to her, she turned to the other cages.

The woman unlocked each door while the boy set a small food plate and a cup of water inside. The woman was careful to lock each door before moving on to the next cage.

"That is so gross," Sophie said, puffing her cheeks as if she was about to vomit. "I don't like other people touching my food."

"More for me," Parker said without missing a beat.

Max watched the giants as they worked their way around the circle. They had reached Axel's cage when Max carefully and quietly slipped off his shoes.

"What are you doing?" Violet whispered, noticing the movement.

"Shh! I have a plan." Max placed a finger to his lips.

The giants were now standing in front of their cage. "Move back, fairy," the boy growled at Max.

Max silently moved as the door was pulled open. The giant plopped the food plate down into the middle of the cage. Not noticing the shoe, he set the water cup directly on top of it. The cup leaned sideways, spilling most of the contents onto the cage floor.

"You idiot," the woman said, slapping the boy's head.

A loud growl came from the ledge. The boy looked up quickly, afraid the dragons were about to swoop down on him. He wiped at the mess with his sleeve, succeeding only in making a bigger mess. Max took that moment to push his other shoe up against the doorframe.

"Leave it," the woman told the boy.

The boy pulled his arm out just as the woman pushed the door shut, twisting the key in the lock before moving on. The boy gave one more hurried look up at the ledge; a single dragon glared down at him.

"That was your great plan?" Violet whispered. "A water spill?"

Max shook his head, "Wait until

they leave."

Parker was already shoving a handful of bread into her mouth.

"You have some serious issues," Sophie said, shaking her head.

Parker made a face as she grabbed another handful of bread, dramatically shoving it into her already full mouth.

Finally, the giants took their tray and disappeared back into the darkness. Max hurried to the cage door, praying for a miracle.

Grasping the bars, he gave them a shove, holding back a cheer of delight when the door swung open.

"How did you do that?" Parker asked, swallowing the last of her bread. "I tried everything!"

"I put my shoe in the way," Max said,

holding up his shoe before sliding it back onto his foot. "Luckily, the first shoe caused the water spill. I was able to get the other one in place while they were distracted with the cleanup. The shoe kept the door from latching properly."

"Sneaky," Parker said, giving her brother a high five.

"Queen Buttercup," Pixie whispered. She flew out of the cage and up to where the queen was being held. She gasped in horror. The queen was lying motionless on the floor of her prison. "Your Majesty!"

"Pixie, look out!" Max shouted a moment later. "Dragon!"

Pixie looked up just in time to see a dragon plummeting down from the ledge, heading straight toward her. She managed to duck underneath the cage seconds before the dragon swiped its claw into the space she had just left. The tip of one of the dragon's talons skimmed the side of the cage, causing it to rock violently back and forth.

The dragon looked up at Pixie from where it stood below her. Pixie's heart skipped a beat. There was nowhere to go. The dragon stood between Pixie and her cage; she would never make it back.

"We have to do something!" Violet cried out.

"I'm thinking! I'm thinking!" Max waved his hands as if to quiet everyone.

"Hey! You! Dragon!" Parker flew out of the cage, yelling at the dragon below her.

"Parker, what are you doing?!" Sophie screamed. "Get back in here!"

Parker ignored her sister and zigzagged quickly over the dragon's head. It worked.

The dragon turned its head toward Parker.

"Parker, go back!" Pixie yelled.

Just then, another dragon swooped down from its perch, heading straight for Parker.

Chapter Six

The Dragon's Lullaby

"Parker, look out!" Sophie yelled.

Max flew out of the cage and barreled into Parker, sending them both flying out of the path of the oncoming dragon.

The two dragons collided, crashing to the floor, roaring, and biting each other.

Pixie took that moment to fly back into the cage with Violet and Sophie.

"Where are Max and Parker?" Sophie "desperately searched the ground.

"There!" Violet shouted, pointing to the opposite side of the room.

Max and Parker pressed themselves flat against the wall, watching the dragons fight just a few feet in front of them.

"I guess that wasn't my best idea," Parker whispered to her brother. "Sorry."

"You were only trying to help." Max sighed.

"Do you think dragons eat fairies?" Parker asked, a tremble in her voice. "I mean, is that why they dive-bombed Pixie?"

"Let's hope not," Max said, although he wondered the same thing. "We should make a dash for it while those two are busy fighting."

Max spoke too soon. A third dragon flew down and landed between the two fighting dragons, forcing them apart.

"Now what?" Parker asked.

"Stay down and stay quiet," Max said. "Hopefully, they'll get bored and go back up."

The third, larger dragon made clicking and clucking sounds, attracting the attention of the two smaller dragons. They both stopped fighting and turned their attention toward the bigger dragon.

"Are they talking to each other?" Violet asked, back in the cage.

"Yes, but I don't know what they're saying," Pixie confessed. "I think she's scolding the younger two."

"She? How do you know it's a girl?" Violet asked.

"The female clicks have a higher pitch," Pixie explained. "Plus, the females are a lighter blue than the males. It's always a little hard to tell at this age, though."

"This age?" Violet asked.

"Yes. Those two are baby dragons," Pixie stated as if it were a well-known fact.

"These are babies?" Sophie questioned in disbelief. "They're so big!"

"Maybe two or three years old," Pixie corrected herself. "All dragons are born black; they change different shades of blue as they get older. The female is closer to your age. Her scales are more blueish."

The girls nodded, fascinated by this information.

"Anyway, their age is probably why the giants can control them," Pixie said.

Violet began to softly sing *Twinkle, Twinkle Little Star*.

"Are you singing? Now?" Sophie asked in disbelief.

Violet nodded as she sang louder, motioning for Sophie to join in.

Sophie felt a bit silly but joined in anyway. When they finished the song, Violet began singing *You Are my Sunshine*. Sophie gave her sister a strange look but continued to follow along. Excitedly, Violet pointed down at the dragons as she continued to sing.

Sophie looked down. Sure enough, the dragons had stopped moving and clicking at each other. Their ears perked up as they listened to the girls singing.

The female dragon nudged the smaller two, who both let out large yawns. With one more nudge, the two males flew back up to the ledge, where they promptly stretched out and lay down.

The female dragon opened her mouth, releasing a loud sigh, before plopping down on the floor below them. Instantly, her eyes shut, and her breathing became heavy.

Max made eye contact with Violet and gave her the thumbs-up sign. Quickly, he and Parker flew back into the safety of the cage.

"Okay, I'll admit that was mostly my fault," Pixie said, turning to Parker. "Thank you for saving me."

"That was pretty scary," Parker said. "I should probably learn to think things through."

"You were only trying to save me," Pixie told her. "Reactions like that aren't always meant to be thought through."

"Although, you could have gotten hurt or killed." Sophie quickly pointed out.

"True, but she succeeded in distracting the dragon and saving me," said Pixie.

"It all worked out in the end. I am worried about Queen Buttercup, though. She doesn't look well. She's pale and just lying there."

"We need a plan," Max said.

"What kind of magic do fairies have?" Violet asked. "It must be pretty powerful if the giants are willing to steal for it."

"The giants have some power of their own," Pixie said. "Our magic combined would make them stronger."

"What kind of magic is it?" Parker raised an eyebrow. "Can you make these cages disappear?"

"No, it's basic fairy magic," Pixie told her. "We make things grow."

"Can you make a key grow?" Parker asked.

"We can't make something out of nothing," Pixie said, shaking her head. "We make plants and flowers grow from seeds or other flowers."

"That's not very useful," Max said. "I can do that."

"We can make it happen faster," Pixie told him. "I can touch a flower bud, and it will immediately blossom."

"We can move things, too," Axel called out from his cage. "Small branches, twigs, leaves, that sort of thing."

"Like telekinesis?" Parker's eyes widened.

Parker's siblings all whipped their heads around to look at her.

"How do you know that word?" Max asked.

"I know a lot of things." Parker shrugged.

"What is tel-a-ka-knees?" Pixie asked.

"Tel-a-ka-knee-sis," Parker corrected. She stated proudly, "It's a term meaning you can move things with your mind."

"I suppose that's what we do," Pixie said.

"Can you move a key?" Max questioned, lifting a finger as an idea brewed.

Pixie pursed her lips together in thought, "If we work together, we should be able to move something that size."

The sound of voices echoed through the cavern. "The giants are coming back," Max said. "This could be our chance."

Chapter Seven

A Giant Surprise

"We need to get that key without the giants noticing," Max said.

"How do we do that?" Pixie asked.

"I'm still working on that part," Max mumbled.

"Time to get more magic." The female giant stepped into view, rubbing her hands together.

As she stepped toward Axel's cage, her foot caught on something. "What is this?"

she asked sharply, gripping the boy's shoulder as she tripped forward.

The boy managed to keep them both from falling. He glanced down at the floor, taking a quick step back. "It's a dragon."

"I know it's a dragon, nincompoop," she said harshly, whacking him on the arm. "Why is it on the floor?"

"Maybe it fell?" the boy said, taking another step back from the sleeping dragon.

"You really are dense," the woman snapped, thrusting out her hand. "Give me the key to this cage."

The boy ducked, believing she would strike him again. Realizing she only wanted the key, he fumbled in his pocket to retrieve it. She snatched it from his hand and unlocked Axel's cage. Keeping one eye on the dragon, she yanked Axel out.

Eager to get to work and distracted by the sleeping dragon, she locked the cage but forgot to take the key.

"She left the key in the lock," Max whispered, pointing excitedly. "This is our chance. While the giants are busy, we need to get the key over here without them noticing. We can hide it until they leave. Then we'll be able to unlock all the cages and free the fairies."

"I'll need a little help," Pixie told him. "I'll fly over to the next cage. That should be enough magic. Keep a lookout and whistle if either giant moves back this way."

Pixie opened the door just enough to squeeze through and flew over to the next cage, careful not to be seen by the giants.

"Hi," she said, peering in. "I need your help moving this key over to my cage."

Five fairies turned to look at her, excitement dancing in their eyes.

"Pixie, are you all right?" one fairy asked. "That dragon almost caught you."

"I'm fine." Pixie waved their questions away. "Listen, we have to move this key while the giants are distracted."

The fairies nodded their heads.

Pixie counted down from five, and the fairies concentrated on moving the large key.

Nothing happened. The key didn't even jiggle.

"Concentrate harder," Pixie hissed, glancing nervously toward the giants.

The fairies tried again, staring harder at the key. Max exchanged a worried look with his sisters.

Suddenly Parker jumped up and pointed wildly, "It's moving!"

The key wiggled, slowly moving backward out of the latch. As soon as it was free of the lock, the key began to seesaw. Pixie quickly flew underneath it, using her hands to steady it.

Parker kept a watchful eye on the giants, who were deep in concentration, mumbling to each other as they moved things around on the table.

As the key neared their cage, Max flew out to help guide it between the bars. "Grab the end as it comes through," he whispered to his sisters.

Violet and Sophie grabbed the key's end, pulling it while Max pushed from the side and Pixie from behind.

The fairies across from them let out soft cheers, waving their fists in the air in quiet celebration as the key safely landed inside the cage.

"Hide it under that plate of food," Sophie said urgently.

Pixie flew back into the cage. Max was about to follow her when he saw the giants moving from the table, heading back in their direction. Quickly, he ducked under the cage pressing himself as flat as possible to the bottom, praying he was out of sight.

The female forgot all about the sleeping dragon and managed to trip over it a second time.

"Stupid dragon," she said, this time kicking the dragon's side.

The dragon woke with a start, automatically flying up into the air and knocking into the giant. The force caused the woman to fall backward, landing on the floor with a thud. Her hood fell from her face, and she looked up with eyes blazing at the dragon.

The children all gasped in surprise. The giant was Krystal, Santa's sister from the North Pole, the one who'd put a spell on the elves!

"You idiot!" Krystal yelled, swinging her hand to smack the dragon.

The dragon flew backward quickly to avoid being hit, crashing into the cage Max was hiding under. The unlocked door flung open as it swung back and forth. The girls inside clung onto the bars to keep from falling out.

Max was tossed from his hiding spot and desperately fluttered in the air, searching for a place to hide. The dragon flew around the room, slightly disoriented, smacking into Max and knocking him off balance.

In his panic, Max lost his concentration and began falling straight toward Krystal.

Krystal looked up at that exact moment to see the falling fairy. She reached out her hand and caught him.

"How did you get out?" she asked, sending a shiver up Max's spine. "I could have sworn I locked that cage."

Clutching Max in her fist, Krystal crawled on her knees, scanning the ground for the missing key.

"Where is the key? You lazy dragon! This is all your fault!" she shouted before turning to the boy. "Kyle, find me that key before all these fairies escape."

Kyle, the boy giant, came rushing over, dropping to his knees to scan the floor beside the woman.

"You are useless." Krystal reached over

and smacked Kyle on the side of his head.

The dragon made a low growl before flying directly at Kyle and Krystal. Kyle ducked in fear as the dragon flew over his head, knocking Krystal flat on her back.

The dragon bared its teeth at Krystal, who held up both her hands in defense. Max fell from her palm, landing on the floor beside her.

Quickly, Max shook himself off and stood up, knowing he had to get out of there. Using all his concentration, he pictured himself flying and lifted off the ground. Max was directly above the dragon when it suddenly reached out and snatched him in its claws. Max didn't have time to react as the dragon lifted him higher and higher into the air; they were headed toward the ledge.

"Max!" Sophie screamed, watching

helplessly as her brother was carried away.

The dragon reached the top of the ledge and dropped Max. In an instant, he was surrounded by several dragons, all looking down at him. He gulped and took a small step back, finding himself teetering dangerously close to the edge.

Chapter Eight

Stealing Magic

"Bring that fairy back this instant!" Krystal yelled.

When the dragons ignored her, she whirled back to her table in frustration. "I'm gonna need more magic," she muttered through clenched teeth. "I'm losing control of those stupid, scaly creatures."

Krystal grabbed Axel and quickly tied him onto a chair.

Placing her hands on either side of the trembling fairy, she murmured words no one could understand.

Immediately, the floor and walls of the cave began to shake as if an earthquake had struck. A loud, rumbling roar echoed throughout the room. The cages swung violently back and forth.

"I think I'm gonna be sick," Sophie muttered, having hardly recovered from the cage swinging moments earlier.

"Yee-haw!" Parker was enjoying the ride.

Up on the ledge, Max was knocked off his feet by the shaking. Forgetting he could fly, he desperately tried to grip onto the hard rocks, but the vibration made it impossible. He slid to the end of the ledge, trying to concentrate on flying, but all he could think about was falling.

Suddenly claws wrapped around his body and pulled him to safety, holding him gently until the walls stopped moving.

Back on the ground, Krystal released her grip on Axel, and everything was still. The tiny fairy slumped forward in his chair. Krystal threw her head back in laughter, sparks of color dancing from her fingertips.

"So that's how she gets the magic," Sophie said.

"We have to stop her," said Violet. "For good this time."

"It will be much harder now that she's a giant," Parker pointed out. "Why did she turn herself into a giant anyway?"

"I hope Max is okay up there." Sophie scanned the ledge for her brother. "Max?"

Max peered over the ledge and waved down at his sisters. Tentatively, he reached out to pat his new dragon friend on its belly. Much to his surprise, the dragon started to laugh. Finding the laugh hilarious, Max continued to stroke the stomach. The dragon's laugh was contagious, and Max found himself laughing as well. A few other dragons wanted their bellies tickled too, which led to more laughter.

"What are you doing up there, dragons?" Krystal bellowed, hearing the commotion.

The dragons continued laughing and playing, ignoring Krystal.

"Those stupid creatures," Krystal muttered.

Parker laughed as the sound of the dragons playing echoed throughout the cave.

"What are you laughing at, fairy?" Krystal demanded, heading back to stand in front of their cage.

Parker stopped laughing and backed up as Krystal's face loomed before her.

"There's my key. You little thieves," Krystal spat out, grabbing the cage in her hands. "Tried to trick me?"

Krystal unhooked the cage from its perch and carried it back to her table. The unlocked door flew open as she tossed it down haphazardly.

Unprepared, Sophie, Violet, Parker, and Pixie rolled out of the cage, landing in a heap on the tabletop. The plate of food slid out behind them, slipping off the table to land, right side up, on the floor.

Krystal managed to catch the key as it bounced out of the cage.

"Kyle, bring me the rest of the fairies," she demanded, handing him the key. "I'll take

their magic and teach those dragons a lesson once and for all."

Krystal turned back to the girls on the table. With one wave of her hand, a rope appeared and tied itself around them. They watched helplessly as Kyle handed Krystal more and more fairies, who were bound together in a long line down the length of the table.

"We have to do something," Parker whispered.

"What can we do?" Sophie asked. "We can't go up against giants. Look at us! We're tiny!"

Violet started to laugh.

"What could possibly be so funny at a time like this?" Sophie demanded.

"I completely forgot that we're tiny," Violet said, rolling her eyes at herself.

"That's exactly my point," Sophie said in exasperation. "We're tiny."

"We aren't *really* tiny, though," Violet tried again. "Krystal isn't *really* a giant. We're just small. But we aren't *really* small."

Sophie gave her sister a strange look.

"You aren't explaining it very well." Parker shook her head at Violet. "We shrunk down when we came through the fairy door. If we can change back to our normal size, we might have a chance."

"Oh." Sophie finally understood. "That's right. Everything looks big because we shrunk down."

"Exactly," Violet said before turning to Pixie. "Can you make *us* grow?"

"Maybe, but it's going to take all the fairy magic we can get," Pixie told them. "If we can grow flowers, maybe we can grow humans too."

"Just don't give me any petals," Parker said in disgust.

Pixie laughed and said with a wink, "I make no promises." Then she turned to the fairy on her right. "Pass this message down the line, 'We need to make them big again.'"

In a game of telephone, the fairies passed the message down the line, one fairy whispering to the next.

"You want us to make friends with a bear?" the fairy at the very end asked loudly, clearly confused.

"Well, that didn't work." Sophie rolled her eyes.

"We need to make them big again," Pixie yelled down the line, gesturing toward Violet, Sophie, and Parker.

"Stop that squawking!" Krystal

demanded.

"She can't even understand us," Parker sighed. "We've been whispering for nothing."

Pixie shrugged, then turned toward the other fairies as best she could. "Okay, on the count of three, use your magic to grow these kids to their normal size."

The fairies all nodded in agreement.

"Ready?" asked Pixie. "One. Two. Three!"

Chapter Nine

Human-Sized Plan

A faint buzzing sound tickled their ears, and as if on a Ferris wheel, the girls felt themselves rising upward. The ropes tightened around their chests, straining against the pressure until they finally broke apart, freeing them.

As the girls grew, they pushed against the other fairies. Sophie jumped to the floor, realizing the fairies at the end of the line sat precariously near the edge of the table. Violet and Parker scooted off next to her.

Krystal turned at the sound. Her eyes widened, and she gasped in astonishment at the sight of the sisters growing right before her eyes.

"Y-you?" she stuttered, recognizing the girls from the North Pole. "How did you get here?" she asked, whipping her head from left to right.

"We were fairies." Parker shrugged, pointing to the empty spots on the table behind her. "Ah man, my wings are gone."

Kyle cowered away from them. Sophie was surprised to find he was only a few inches taller than her.

"A little help up here," Max called down from the ledge. He had grown back to his usual height as well. "How do I get down? I lost my wings."

At his normal size, the dragons were only about the size of a Husky, and they were just as slobbery. They licked at his face and arms.

"You can't stop me." Krystal sneered at the girls in front of her. "You couldn't at the North Pole, and you won't be able to here. I'm too powerful."

Krystal opened her palm to reveal Queen Buttercup lying there. Gently, she set the pale, sickly queen on the table.

"What have you done to her?" Violet gasped.

"I've taken her magic," Krystal said coolly. "There is just enough left to help me extract the magic from the rest of these fairies. Then, *I* will rule Emerald Valley. I already know how to control these dragons; perhaps I'll take over the Valley of Fire as well."

"You aren't taking any more magic,"

98

Parker announced, taking a step forward.

"Get out of my way," Krystal said, shoving Parker.

Parker stumbled backward and, unable to catch herself, fell to the floor with a thump.

Krystal grasped the queen, mumbling quietly once again. Like before, there was a loud rumbling sound, and the floor shook violently. The movement knocked Violet and Sophie into one another as they struggled to keep their balance and stay upright.

"Look," Violet said, pointing to Krystal. "The ring on Krystal's finger is glowing. That must be where the magic is kept."

"We need to get that ring," Parker said, trying to push herself up from the floor.

"Look out below!" Max shouted from above them.

Max headed straight for Krystal, riding on

the back of a dragon. The dragon dove directly at Krystal, knocking her off her feet. As she fell, she released her hold on Queen Buttercup, and the room went still.

"Grab that dragon," Krystal yelled at Kyle.

Kyle backed farther into the corner, trying to hide. Violet took her chance to charge at Krystal. Krystal had just pushed herself up onto her hands and knees when Violet crashed into her, causing them both to tumble across the floor.

"Get off me!" Krystal shouted, shoving Violet away.

Krystal attempted to push herself up once again. The dragon circled over her and landed on her back, forcing her down onto her stomach. The dragon squawked in triumph as Max slid off its back.

"Get this dragon off me!" Krystal

screamed in frustration. "Kyle! So, help me, if you don't do something, I will make you pay!"

The dragon began to nip at Krystal's head, causing her to scream out. Violet took that moment to crawl over, grab Krystal's hand, and yank the ring from her finger.

"Give that back to me," Krystal demanded, struggling to shake the dragon from her back.

Violet gave the dragon a quick pat on its leathery head as she hurried toward the table. Setting the ring down, she picked up the empty cage and slammed it down, shattering the ring into tiny pieces.

Wisps of smoke in all different colors oozed from the shards of the broken ring. The smoke whirled around Queen Buttercup, lifting her up in the air and turning her slowly around.

The queen took in a sharp breath and opened her eyes. Gently, the whirling smoke set the queen upright on the table. The smoke continued to circle around the standing queen, whirling and whirling until it disappeared inside her.

"Wow!" Violet gasped.

Queen Buttercup looked up at Violet. "Thank you. You saved me. You saved us all." She took a moment to recover before turning her gaze to Krystal.

"You stole my magic!" Queen Buttercup shouted, her eyes blazing. "You almost killed my fairies for your own personal gain, and you tried to destroy our home." Queen Buttercup waved her hands around in a circle and aimed them at Krystal.

Instantly, Krystal was bound by

shimmering ropes.

"Let me go!" Krystal demanded.

"No! You are hereby banished from this land." Queen Buttercup pointed a finger at Krystal. "You will live out the rest of your days imprisoned in the Valley of Fire."

"You can't do that," Krystal spat out.

"I can, and I will," Queen Buttercup replied, then pointed to the dragons above them. "You stole these precious babies from their families and from their land. For that, you must be punished."

Queen Buttercup motioned toward the dragons. "You are all free to go home now. Please take Krystal to the dragon king."

"I won't go," Krystal huffed.

Queen Buttercup fluttered her fingers again, and a gag wrapped around Krystal's mouth. "That is quite enough out of you."

Queen Buttercup took a moment to smooth out her hair before turning toward Kyle. "And you, what do you have to say for yourself? I should imprison you for helping this woman."

The female dragon stepped between Kyle and Queen Buttercup, making a series of clicking and clucking noises.

"Oh, my," Queen Buttercup said, a hand fluttering to her chest. Glancing back at Krystal, she said, "It seems your power over the dragons has little to do with magic and everything to do with this boy."

Kyle was breathing heavily against the wall. "Wh-what do the dragons wa-want with me?" his voice trembled as he spoke.

"Do not be afraid," Queen Buttercup said gently. "The dragons only want to protect you."

"What? Why?" Kyle asked.

"Because you are one of them," Queen Buttercup said. "You are a dragon."

Chapter Ten

Return of the Queen

"I'm a what?" Kyle laughed at the thought. "Those dragons kept trying to bite me!"

"No, they never tried attacking *you*," Queen Buttercup told him. "They only attacked Krystal. They tried to protect you from her. Krystal made you think you were a human. She held you captive and used you to control the dragons." She turned toward the female dragon. "This is Raina, your sister."

Raina took a step toward Kyle, but he refused to move away from the wall.

"She won't hurt you," Max promised.

Kyle stood in place as the dragon approached him, rubbing her head against his arm. He shrank against the wall, still not trusting the dragons weren't going to hurt him.

"Your name is actually Enda," Queen Buttercup said. "You are the youngest son of the Dragon King."

"You're a prince?" Violet said. "Cool!"

Kyle looked confused.

"I know it's difficult to understand," Queen Buttercup said softly.

Kyle's heart was racing as the large dragon continued rubbing her head against him. Queen Buttercup gave him an encouraging smile. Placing her arms in front of her, she moved her fingers swiftly as if playing across an invisible piano. Magically, Kyle transformed from a human back into his dragon form.

Instantly, his memories came rushing back. Raina looked down at her brother. This time Kyle, now Enda, rubbed his face against his sister. Raina clicked a thank you to Queen Buttercup before heading back up to the ledge with Enda in tow.

From the ridge above, Raina made another quick series of clicking noises. The two strongest dragons flew down to Krystal, each grabbing an arm. Together they lifted the kicking and struggled Krystal up toward the ledge. One by one, the dragons disappeared from view, their shadows no longer moving along the walls.

"Where did they go?" Sophie asked.

"Home," Queen Buttercup told her. "The portal to Vatrena Dolena, the land of dragons, is up there."

"I wish I could believe this is the last we'll see of Krystal," Max commented.

"She'll be locked up for a long time," Queen Buttercup promised. "No one has ever escaped from Draconia Prison. She won't be bothering anyone anymore. Now, let's free these fairies and go home."

The children worked their way down the table, untying all the fairies.

Queen Buttercup reached out to touch the side of Axel's face. With a jolt, Axel sat up straight and opened his eyes.

"Your Majesty." he bowed his head as the queen untied him.

Queen Buttercup turned to the children. "I believe it will be easier for everyone if you four can fly back to Emerald Valley."

With a wiggle of her fingers, the children shrank back down. Wings sprouted from their backs once again.

"Yes!" Parker shouted with glee. "I love the flying part!"

Queen Buttercup laughed as Parker soared up into the air, performing a series of flips along the way.

"Follow me, everyone!" Queen Buttercup led the way out of the mountain.

This time, the children had no problems keeping up with the fairies. They burst out of the cave and descended into the valley below.

As they soared through the trees, they heard Queen Buttercup cry out below them, "Emerald Valley!" The queen stood on an uprooted tree, looking sadly at her home.

"We can fix it," Pixie told her, then unsure, "Can't we?"

"I'll need all the fairies' help for this one."

The queen began singing a wordless tune, the melody floating throughout the entire valley.

The children looked at each other in amazement as fairies began pouring out of tree trunks, tree roots, and bushes around the meadow.

"I had no idea there were so many fairies here," Sophie said.

"This is so cool," Violet whispered in awe.

"Everyone, hold hands and join together in the fairy song," Queen Buttercup ordered.

The fairies followed their queen's command, gathering in a circle and joining hands. Pixie reached for Sophie's hand and motioned for the children to join the fairies.

Queen Buttercup closed her eyes and continued to sing, the other fairies joining her in song. The air filled with the most beautiful music the children had ever heard.

"It sounds like harps and windchimes," Sophie commented.

"Everything is changing." Parker whipped her head around to watch.

Everything *was* changing. Water rushed back down the dried riverbed, filling the lake with clear, blue-green water. The brown moss turned a vibrant green, covering the valley in what looked like a thick, emerald carpet.

The burnt trees came back to life, standing tall, green buds blossoming from their branches. Flowers rose from beneath small patches of grass all around the meadow.

Emerald Valley sparkled once more.

"Now, *this* looks more like an emerald valley," Parker laughed.

"Now we celebrate!" Pixie shouted. Turning to the children, she asked, "Will you stay for the party?"

"We love a good party," Sophie said.

"Especially if there's food," Parker agreed.

The children stayed with the fairies long into the evening. They feasted on berries sweeter than they'd ever dreamed, swam in the river, ziplined over the uprooted tree trunks, and explored the fairy homes.

As the sun began to set in the distance, the children knew it was time to go.

"I don't want to leave," Violet whined.

"Being a fairy is amazing," Parker said, with one more flip in the air.

Sadly, it was time to say goodbye to Queen Buttercup and all the fairies. With dragging feet, they followed Pixie back to the ravine.

"Ready for one last flight?" Pixie asked.

Together, they all flew up and out of the valley, weaving back and forth through the forest until they reached the avenue of trees that would lead them home.

"Race ya!" Parker yelled as she burst down the avenue at full speed.

They were all laughing by the time they reached the oak tree. The fairy door still hung low on the trunk. The magic cube rested in the grass beside the door.

"Let's do this," Max said, picking up the cube. He pushed the buttons, flipped the switches, and pulled the lever.

They all turned and hugged Pixie one last time.

"Thank you for an amazing adventure," Sophie said.

"Thank you for saving Emerald Valley," Pixie replied.

Max pulled open the fairy door. The children walked through the door one by one, transforming back to their original size as they passed through.

"I'm gonna miss having wings," Parker said sadly.

"There's Mom and Dad." Sophie pointed out. "It's like we never left."

"Just like last time, we've been gone all day, but no time has passed here," Violet said.

"The last one to the slide is a rotten egg!" Max yelled.

The children took off, running toward the playground. Eagar to win the race, Max didn't realize he no longer held the magic cube.

The End

Thank you for taking the time to read *"Journey Through the Fairy Door."* I hope you enjoyed the story.

I love writing the Magic Cube Adventures and would love to share these books with readers everywhere. As a self-published author, reviews are the best way to show others how much you enjoyed a book. If you liked this book, it would be fantastic if you would give it a rating on Amazon and/or GoodReads. If you leave a short review, that would be helpful as well.

https://www.amazon.com/Journey-Through-Fairy-Door-Magic/dp/1736065610

> **Writing a Simple Review:**
>
> *Pick one or all options below:*
>
> A) What was your favorite part of the story?
> B) Who were your favorite characters and why?
> C) Would you recommend this book to others?

Curious where the Magic Cube came from? Join our mailing list to receive exclusive content, including a free, six-chapter Prequel story, the first look at illustrations, cover reveals, chapter excerpts, book recommendations, and more.

www.mitchelmareee.com

Author's Note

Ireland is known for the fairy folk. Called The Sidhe in Irish (pronounced Shee). When we first moved to Dublin, we loved all the fairy doors hanging in trees and gardens around the city.

Ireland is full of fairy trees, fairy villages, and even great mounds of stone walls believed to be ancient homes of the fairy folk.

Inspiration for this book came from finding those fairy doors throughout the city. I wondered what it would be like if we could shrink down and enter through a fairy door. What would be on the other side?

The Adventure Continues Spring 2022

"Everything is pink!" Violet exclaimed, eyes darting from one spot to another in their new location.

Swirling pink cotton covered the landscape before them. Trees, their branches covered in pink clouds, lined the border of the open field they stood in. Pink bushes of thick spun sugar dotted the area. Instead of grass, strings of pink covered the ground.

A thick scent of pure sugar hung in the air.

"It looks like a cotton candy machine exploded," Max commented.

"Do you think it *is* cotton candy?" Parker licked her lips and picked a piece of the pink fluff from the ground.

Sophie sniffed the air a few times. "Smells

like it."

"Tastes like it too." Parker's eyes widened as she licked the pink off her fingers.

"Reminds me of a carnival," Violet said, taking a big sniff.

"I feel like we're in the board game, *Candyland*," Max scrunched up his face and walked through the field.

"I love that game." Parker scanned the ground. "I don't see colored squares, though."

"There's a path over here," Max called, waving his sisters over. "We'd better follow it. Maybe we can figure out what we're doing here."

Follow the Watson's on a tasty adventure through Frosted Falls as they search for the stolen Sapphire Crown.

Acknowledgments

As always, thank you to my wonderful children. Your imaginations are the spark and inspiration for these stories.

Thank you to Kevin for the constant encouragement and support.

Thank you to Wes for encouraging me and critiquing my work.

Thank you to Ola Snimshchikova for once again creating amazing illustrations and a fun cover.

Thank you to Shannon Burns at Wildflower Books for your perfect edits and suggestions.

Thank you to my beta readers for the advice and sometimes difficult criticism I needed to make this story great.

Thank you to Barbara Smith for the final edits.

Thank you to all the parents and teachers who encourage children to pick up a book and escape.

About the Author

Mitchel Maree grew up lost in imaginary worlds. Now, she is taking those adventures and creating magical stories to share with children everywhere. Mitchel loves folklore and legends, especially from Ireland. She loves to weave mythical creatures into her stories.

Mitchel currently resides in Dublin, Ireland with her family. She enjoys spending time outdoors, exploring new places, playing at the beach, and reading mystery novels.

Printed in Great Britain
by Amazon